THE DAY ZOOMBOP
THE SPACE ALIEN
CAME TO MY HOUSE

By Joan Staehle
Illustrated by Bob Staehle

AuthorHouse™
1663 Liberty Drive, Suite 200
Bloomington, IN 47403
www.authorhouse.com
Phone: 1-800-839-8640

First published by AuthorHouse   6/2/2008

ISBN: 978-1-4343-8632-8 (sc)

Printed in the United States of America
Bloomington, Indiana

This book is printed on acid-free paper.

authorHOUSE®

This book is dedicated to our granddaughter, Penelope,
and to our other little buddies: Hannah, Adam, Dallas and Rachel.

It was a regular crummy old day when Zoombop the space alien came to my house. I had to get up early that morning because my silly bird was whistling so loud it sounded like he was going to break the windows in our house. I gave him a mirror so he could look at himself. He was so impressed that he got totally quiet again. (He sure likes himself!)

    Well, as I said, it was just a regular old day. Oh, except, did I mention that it was Saturday? Well, it *was* Saturday. So the rest of the people in my family were still asleep.

    Just to make sure my annoying little sister wasn't up sneaking around the house, I checked our back porch. That's where my sister keeps her doll house. Sometimes she crawls out of bed early on a Saturday morning and plays with her doll house. Who knows what she pretends?

    I can't imagine playing with anything so boring as a doll house. Anyhow, she wasn't on the porch.

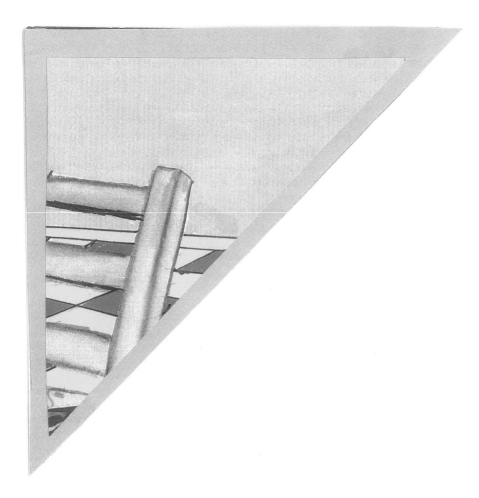

No one else in my house was out of bed yet, so I tip-toed into the kitchen. I poured a tall glass of milk and only spilled a small puddle of it. I sawed off a giant chunk of chocolate cake. I ate the cake with my hands and stuffed Tyrannosaurus-size bites of it into my mouth. Sweet, gooey frosting stuck to my two front teeth and squished out of the gap where my bottom tooth is missing. Some frosting snuck up my nose and tried to smother me. I sipped cold milk to clear my airways.

(When you are the only one up on a Saturday morning, you have to be very safety-conscious while eating your breakfast.)

After I finished my breakfast I skipped outside and looked at my red bicycle. My bike is shiny and has a basket for carrying things. I didn't feel like riding my bike, though. It might be boring. Instead, I checked inside our mailbox. The flag was up, but there was no mail inside the box.

The only thing in the mailbox was a pair of enormous staring eyeballs. Those eyeballs looked like two spotlights with glowing oranges in the middles of them. They were staring right at me.

So, I closed the door on the mailbox.

    I went straight to our backyard and climbed the ladder to my tree house.

    Some days I pretend that my tree house is a nest up in the branches of the world's tallest tree. I pretend I am up above the rest of the world and my sharp eyes can see everything everyone does everywhere. (No one can see me up in my tree house, of course.)

    But right then it was not time for pretending. It was time for thinking. I thought, and thought, and thought. I thought about those two enormous eyes peering out of our mailbox.

Suddenly I got an idea. Maybe those eyeballs weren't *eyeballs* at all. Maybe they were two round balloons. Maybe someone had gotten two round balloons at a birthday party. Maybe someone had stuffed two balloons into our mailbox to play a trick on me.

Slowly I climbed back down the ladder. Ever so stealthily, I crept toward our front yard. I padded down our driveway until I reached the mailbox. Ever so carefully I pulled open the door on the mailbox and looked in again.

This time I saw....nothing! Only black emptiness stared back at me.

Where had those balloons gone? Had they floated away?

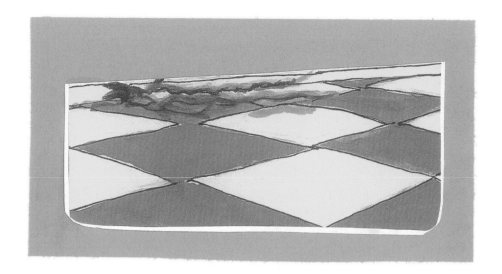

Then a screechy squealing honking sound attacked my ears. It sounded like the king of all geese honking a warning to all the geese of the world: "Ssssnock! Ssssnock!"

Maybe a goose was sliding in spaghetti across a slippery kitchen floor. (I did that one time.)

But there was no goose and no slippery floor.

What was making that horrible noise? And why did it sound like it was coming from my tree house?

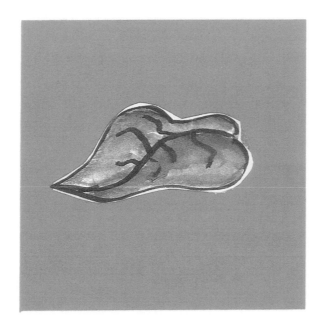

I raced back to the tree house to check it out. When I climbed to the top of the ladder and peeked over the edge of a branch, there sat a slurping purplish space alien with enormous bulging eyeballs.

As soon as he saw me, he made the most horrible screeching squealing honking sound you ever did hear: "Ssssnock! Ssssnock!"

I was so surprised that I fell off of the ladder and landed on the ground on my backside. My underwear got twisted into a bundle from the fall.

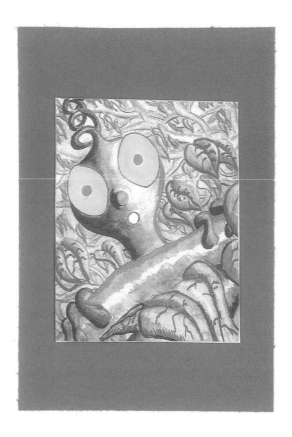

When I raised my head up off of the ground, there he was, peering over the edge of a branch.

"Who are *you*?" I asked.

"I'm Zoombop," he answered. "I'm not from around here."

"I didn't think you were," I replied. "Where *are* you from?"

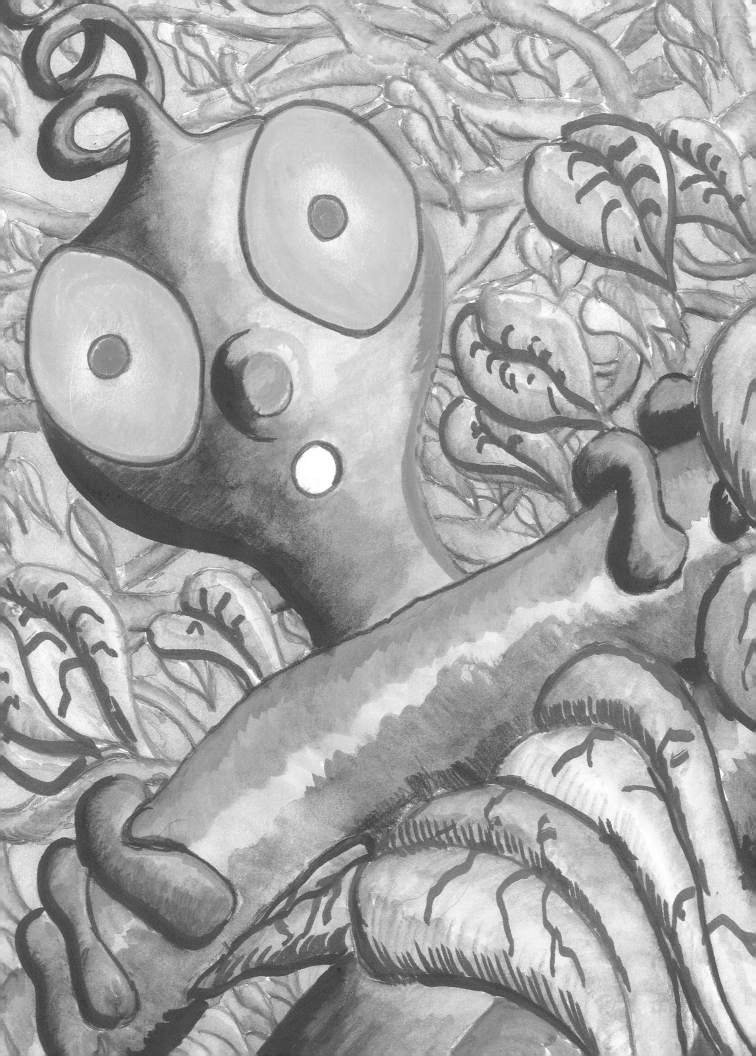

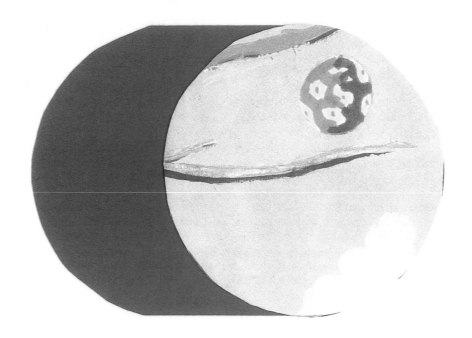

Zoombop floated down to the ground beside me. He scratched the squiggly curlicue that grew out of the top of his head. The curlicue straightened out into an arrow that pointed up through the branches of the tree to the sky beyond. "Zimtup," he said. "I come from Zimtup."

My parents were still asleep. Zoombop opened the door
to their bedroom and floated in. I walked heel-toe, heel-toe
like an Indian scout sneaking through a forest.

When I reached their bedside I yelled: "Hey, Mom! Hey,
Dad! Can my friend Zoombop stay for lunch today?"

Dad just groaned.

Mom pulled a pillow over her head.

My parents looked pretty funny. Their hair was sticking
out all over their heads like hay in a hurricane. They were in
a big jumble of wrinkled pajamas, sheets, and blankets. Dad
made some smacking noises with his lips but didn't say any
real words.

Can he? Can Zoombop stay for lunch?" I pleaded.

"Sure," Dad said without opening his eyes.

"Anything. Whatever," Mom mumbled from under her
pillow.

Mom made my favorite lunch: mashed potatoes and spaghetti with meatballs. Zoombop put salt in his milk. He tied a long spaghetti strand around the curlicue on his head. He opened secret pouches on his knees and put extra meatballs inside (for later, I guess.)

Mom and Dad sure were surprised!

After lunch Zoombop and I sailed my toy sailboat on the fish pond in my backyard. Zoombop tried sailing my mother's iron, but it sank. I guess it was too heavy or something. Zoombop said something about *density and displacement*. I just nodded. I decided to ask my parents about those words later.

The day was almost over. Zoombop and I went back into my house through my back porch. My sister was there playing with her doll house. Zoombop wanted to play too.

The three of us played and played. My sister and I pretended we were little mice living in the doll house. Zoombop pretended he was a tweekthump. Do you know what a *tweekthump* is? I don't know either, but tweekthumps seem to be able to stand on one hand on top of a dollhouse.

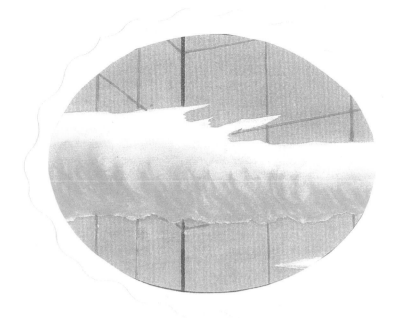

At bath time, Zoombop and I made mountains of bubbles in the bathtub and played with my toy ship. When I finally started letting the water out of the tub, Zoombop was afraid he might go down the drain with the water and the bubbles. I told him I thought he would be safe because I had never gone down the drain yet, and I have taken LOTS of baths.

That night Zoombop and I went into my sister's room so we could see the moon. Zoombop very kindly turned my sister's doll and stuffed animals around so they could look out of the window too. We all sat silently for a long time. We just looked at the round white moon and the stars that were dancing around cheering up the night sky.

Finally Zoombop said: "Tomorrow I must return to Zimtup. Do you want to go with me?"

"Maybe some day, but not tomorrow," I said. My bird sings for me every morning, and he would miss me if I were gone. I promised my sister we could use my action figures in her doll house tomorrow. I really need to ride my bike or it might rust just sitting around without being used. And my parents need me to fix healthy breakfasts on Saturdays and check the mailbox each day."

"Well, maybe I'll come back again and you can go to Zimtup with me then," offered Zoombop. "Zimtup is a VERY interesting place."

"Next time I might go with you," I agreed, "but I think Earth is a VERY interesting place too."

What was your favorite part of this book? Why did you like that part?

Language and Memory Skill Development

Ask your child to look at the page of reduced pictures from this story of Zoombop and retell the story in his/her own words using the small pictures as references for retelling the story.

Reinforcing Color Recognition Skills

Ask: Can you find something in this book that is:

red?	orange?	yellow?	green?	blue?	purple?
black?	white?	pink?	brown?	gray?	

Practicing Counting Skills and Comparisons

Help your child find the answers to these questions.
Practice counting the items together:

How many ships are in the bathtub?
How many fish are in the pond?
How many fingers are on one of Zoombop's hands?
How many blades are on the ceiling fan?
Let's count the small (reduced) illustrations together.

How many pictures of Zoombop can you find in this book?

Which are there more of in this book: small illustrations or
large ones?

Identifying Shapes

Help your child practice identifying shapes by asking:
Can you look through the pictures in this book and find examples of each of these shapes?

circle   oval   square   rectangle   star   heart   triangle

Developing Analytical Skills

Encourage your child to discuss these ideas:

Could a bird whistle loud enough to break a window?
Would chocolate cake be a good breakfast? Why/Why not?
What do you think is the best color for a bike? Why?
Do you think Zoombop would be a good friend to have?
What are two of your favorite foods? What do you like about
    those foods?

Encouraging Appreciation for Literature

What do you think was the funniest part of this book?
If you found Zoombop in your mailbox, what would you do?
How did you feel when Zoombop said he must return to
    Zimtup?

Responding to Literature Creatively

Draw a picture of what you might find if you went with
Zoombop to Zimtup.

Write a story about finding something funny in your mailbox. Here are
some ideas for items which might be unusual to find in a mailbox: a toad, a
mysterious note, an old gold coin, a pen that writes words backwards.

Make a list of things you would *like* to find in your
mailbox.

Make another list of things you would *not* want to find in
your mailbox.

Silently act out these verbs from the story of Zoombop:

sneaking	*playing*	*tip-toeing*	*pouring*	*sawing*
sipping	*staring*	*closing*	*climbing*	*thinking*
pulling	*floating*	*peeking*	*pointing*	*pleading*

Practice letter recognition, alphabetical order and phonics by pointing to these letters and words and reading them aloud as your child repeats them after you:

A a	animals alien asleep arrow
B b	bird balloons bike bed bubbles
C c	cake curlicue chocolate
D d	doll day door driveway drain Dad
E e	else enormous early
F f	family frosting flag front floor fall
G g	goose geese ground go gooey gap
H h	house hair head hay hurricane
I i	Indian iron if interesting
J j	jumble
K k	kindly kitchen king
L l	ladder lunch lips later lots
M m	moon mailbox Mom meatballs mumbled
N n	noise nose nest nothing nodded night
O o	oranges over opened outside
P p	porch pillow potatoes parents puddle
Q q	quiet
R r	room ride rust red round
S s	Saturday sound stars spaghetti sky
T t	tip-toed teeth tree toy tweekthump top
U u	underwear up
V v	very
W w	water window world wrinkled words
X x	eXtra
Y y	yelled you
Z z	Zoombop Zimtup

LaVergne, TN USA
10 February 2010
172625LV00005B